BRATZ™

SUPER STARZ MASQUERADE

By Christine Peymani

SCHOLASTIC INC.

New York   Toronto   London   Auckland   Sydney
Mexico City   New Delhi   Hong Kong   Buenos Aires

ISBN-13: 978-0-439-91952-4
ISBN-10: 0-439-91952-5

Designed by Jenn Martino

12 11 10 9 8 7 6 5 4 3 2 1   7 8 9 10/0

Printed in the U.S.A.
First printing, October 2007

CHAPTER 1

D id you get your tickets yet?" Cloe asked eagerly as she ran up to her best friends at their lockers after school.

"What tickets?" Jade asked, her green eyes sparkling as she tried to hide her grin. "For the football game? Or that new romantic comedy? Or the museum's special Impressionism exhibit?"

"No!" Cloe cried. "Although, I do want to catch the football game—and the movie—and the exhibit. Did you really get tickets to all of those?"

"Not yet," Jade replied. "But was there something else you were trying to ask about?"

"Oh, right!" Cloe was always getting caught up in her latest idea, which made it hard for her to focus. But her constant stream of new ideas also made her lots of fun. "I was talking about the Masquerade Ball, of course!"

"Oh, the *Masquerade* Ball," Jade said. "I didn't know you wanted to go to that. Did you know that, girls?" She turned to Sasha and Yasmin, who shook their heads slowly, though Yasmin had to put her hand over her mouth to contain her giggles.

Cloe's blue eyes widened. "You did too! We've been talking about this for weeks, and—" She paused, noticing the smiles on her friends' faces. "Oh," she murmured. "You were just kidding."

"Sorry, Cloe," Yasmin said, putting her arm around her friend. "Of course we know how excited you are about this dance."

"Which made it all the easier to tease you about it," Sasha added.

"Okay, ha-ha," Cloe replied. "But seriously, did you get your tickets?"

"Sure did!" Sasha told her as the other girls nodded. "Did you?"

"Um, yeah!" Cloe cried. "I was like, the first one in line this morning. I mean, the dance does sell out every year, and I definitely didn't want to miss out!"

The Stilesville Masquerade Ball was held on Halloween every year, and it was always the town's biggest event.

"Well, our costumes *are* the highlight of the dance every year," Jade pointed out. "We have to be there — it wouldn't be the Stilesville Masquerade Ball without us!"

"It almost doesn't seem fair," Sasha chimed in. "I mean, we win the costume contest every single year. Maybe we *should* take a year off, to give someone else a chance."

"Don't be silly!" Cloe cried. "This is going to be the best Masquerade Ball ever! Mayor Davis is even hiring live musical acts to perform at the dance this year."

"That *will* be great," Sasha agreed.

"But not as great as our costumes!" Jade added.

"Okay, if you're so sure of yourselves, what *are* we going as this year?" Yasmin inquired as she shut her locker and strolled with her three friends toward the door.

Sasha and Jade exchanged glances. "No idea," Jade admitted.

"But I know what I *don't* want to do," Sasha added. "I don't want to go as witches, or vampires, or ghosts. None of that typical Halloween stuff."

"Totally," Jade agreed. "I'm so over all of those creepy costumes. I mean, we've done it all before, you know?"

"Exactly!" Sasha exclaimed. "We need something totally fun, fresh, and upbeat for this year's ball."

"But you have no idea what?" Cloe asked as they burst outside into the crisp autumn afternoon. When Sasha and Jade both shook their heads, she cried, "But Jade, you're our resident *fashionista*! We depend on you to dream up our amazing new looks. And Sasha, you're our organizer extraordinaire. If you don't have a plan, who does?" She stopped in the middle of the parking lot, looking from one friend to the next, waiting for an answer.

"Cloe, it'll be okay," Yasmin began. "Sure, we don't have anything decided yet, but we still have two weeks until the dance."

"Yeah, I've whipped up spectacular outfits in way less time than that," Jade reminded Cloe.

"And don't worry, Cloe," Sasha added. "I do have a plan."

"You do?" Cloe gasped. "What is it? Tell me!"

A wide smile spread across Sasha's face. "I say we hit the mall and get some inspiration there. Who's with me?"

"I am!" her three best friends chorused. They raced each other to Cloe's cruiser and hopped inside, eager for a trip to one of their favorite places, the Stilesville Mall!

* * *

"There's nothing here," Cloe moaned as they trudged out of yet another store. They had checked out all of their favorite shops at the mall but hadn't found anything that was right for the Masquerade Ball.

"I don't get it," Jade said, shaking her head. "We always get tons of awesome ideas at the mall!"

"Maybe we've tapped out these stores," Sasha suggested. "I mean, we *have* been shopping at them for years, and we couldn't expect them to stay on the cutting edge forever."

"Then what are we going to do?" Cloe demanded. She slumped onto a bench, and her friends crowded in beside her, their eyes half-closed with exhaustion.

Yasmin leaned her head against the back of the bench, and that was when she noticed something at the far end of the hallway. "Wait, what's that?" she asked, pointing toward the sign she'd seen.

The girls sat up straighter, squinting in the direction Yasmin had pointed.

"Well, I'm not sure," Jade began. "But I think it's a new store!"

"Let's go find out!" Sasha suggested. All four girls rushed down the hallway, stopping only when they were facing the new store's window display.

"It's beautiful," Cloe sighed.

"'Retro Chick,'" Jade read from the sign above the door. "That sounds perfect!"

"Good find, Yas!" Sasha declared.

"Well, come on, let's go see how good a find it is." Yasmin stepped into the store, and her friends followed, looking from side to side as if they couldn't absorb everything fast enough.

"Check out this incredible top!" Cloe squealed, scooping up a turquoise tank top with gold metallic beading. She held it up and struck a pose. "Wouldn't I look amazing in this?"

"Totally!" Jade agreed. But Sasha shook her head.

"I just don't think it's the right look for the Masquerade Ball," Sasha said. "I mean, what kind of costume would that be?"

"I don't know . . ." Cloe admitted, hanging the shirt back on the rack.

"You could still buy it, even if it's not for a costume!" Yasmin pointed out, picking up the shirt and handing it back to Cloe.

Cloe's eyes lit up. "That's true!" she declared. "I'm getting it!"

"Girls, we need to focus here," Sasha insisted. "This store is our last chance. If we can't find something here, I don't know what we'll do for the dance!"

Yasmin and Cloe nodded seriously and began searching the racks one by one. But Jade had wandered off to the shoe display in the back of the store. Suddenly she squealed, "Girls! I've got it!"

Her three best friends rushed to the shoe section, where they found Jade triumphantly holding up a pair of knee-high boots. "Go-go boots!" she cried.

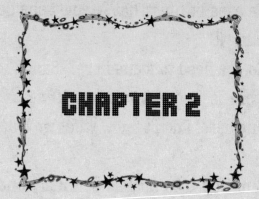

CHAPTER 2

Cloe, Sasha, and Yasmin exchanged confused looks, wondering what Jade was planning for them. "Um . . . so we're going as girls in boots?" Cloe asked uncertainly.

"No!" Jade replied. She held up a matching cream-colored vest that she'd tucked under her arm and waved it above the boots. "We're going as teen pop sensations. Can't you just see it?"

Her friends stared at her, not quite comprehending her vision, but Jade kept talking. "Okay, wait, let me show you the rest." She hurried over to a rack of miniskirts and quickly flipped through them, finally grabbing a short lilac-colored skirt with a ruffled hem and holding it out to the girls.

"So picture this skirt, and—" She darted to a nearby rack of shirts and honed in on one the exact same shade as the skirt. "And this top, with the vest over it, and the boots, of course. Oh, and accessories!"

She dashed to the display of necklaces at the front of the store, her friends trailing behind her with amused looks on their faces. Jade grabbed a long strand of gold beads and looped it around her neck one, two, three times. "And then this would add some sparkle and tie it all together!" she declared.

When her friends still looked unconvinced, she continued, "Maybe you need to see it on." She rushed toward the dressing room with her friends following her.

In the dressing room, Jade changed quickly,

eager to show off her new look to her friends. "You'll love it when you see it all together!" she called over the stall door.

"I'm sure we will," Yasmin agreed, but the girls exchanged uncertain looks.

Suddenly Jade burst out of her fitting room and did a quick little twirl. "Ta-da!" she cried.

"Jade, you look fabulous!" Sasha squealed.

"See, I told you this would work!" Jade replied. "It's modern and fun, with a tinge of disco glam. We'll look like totally spectacular superstars!"

"Love it!" Cloe exclaimed. "Jade, will you help me find my outfit next?"

"Absolutely," Jade agreed. "In fact, I saw a flared fuchsia skirt with black trim that would be perfect for you."

"Ooh, with a matching shirt, right?" Cloe asked. When Jade nodded, Cloe turned and grabbed a fuchsia tee from the shirt rack.

"And don't forget the boots!" Sasha appeared at their sides carrying two pairs of white knee-high boots with gold studs in different patterns. "Which ones do you want, Cloe?"

Cloe reached for the simpler pair, explaining, "I want tons of accessories, so I better not overdo it!" Up front, she found exactly what she was looking for—a skinny black scarf that she looped around her neck, and a gold necklace with sparkly dangles.

Sasha joined her with a short purple dress and matching faux-fur shrug. "Toss in this necklace," Sasha said, picking up a chunky burgundy chain, "and I'm good to go!"

"What about Yasmin?" Cloe asked, noticing that Yasmin still hadn't picked up anything.

The girls hurried to her side, and Yasmin gazed at them sadly. "I can't find any skirts that I like," she explained.

"But this store is awesome!" Cloe protested. "How can you not find anything you like?"

"I found something I like," Yasmin replied. "But I don't think it goes with what you guys picked out."

"Well, let's see it," Sasha told her.

Yasmin led her friends to a rack of blue jeans and pulled out a pair of dark-blue, skinny-fit jeans.

"Hmm," Sasha said. "You're right, they don't really go."

"Hold on," Jade interrupted. "These could look totally hip onstage. We just need the right accessories to make this outfit pop."

She urged her friends back to the front of the store, where she scooped up a floppy lavender hat with a silver band and plopped it on Yasmin's head. "Now that's a good start," Jade declared. She scoped out the accessories for a moment, then settled on a long silver scarf, which she draped around Yasmin's neck.

"Ooh, then what about this, too?" Yasmin asked, grabbing a matching silver belt.

"Perfect!" Jade agreed. "Now we need a lavender top to pull it together." She grabbed Yasmin's hand and pulled her toward the racks of tank tops, where she picked out just the right shade to match the hat.

"Awesome!" Yasmin declared, running her hands over the shirt's soft material.

"Now all you need is boots," Jade added.

In the shoe section, Yasmin went straight for a pair of lavender calf-high boots with white faux-fur trim. "These are gorgeous," she murmured.

"Get 'em!" Jade told her.

The girls hurried to the checkout counter, their arms filled with their new outfits.

"Are you sure Yasmin's outfit will fit into our look?" Sasha whispered to Jade.

"Definitely!" Jade insisted. "Anyway, it's always good to mix it up a little, you know?"

"I guess . . ." Sasha replied, but she didn't sound convinced.

The girls paid for their new threads, then headed for the food court to chill out with some smoothies. They grabbed a table and sprawled into their chairs, their shopping bags piled around them.

"We did it!" Cloe sighed, relieved.

"These *are* cool outfits," Sasha agreed. "But how is anyone going to know we're supposed to be pop stars?"

"Actually," Jade replied with a grin, "I have an idea."

Jade's best friends leaned toward her eagerly, but Jade paused, letting the suspense build. "Come on, spill!" Cloe cried finally. "What's your big idea?"

"Well, you know how the mayor is looking for live music for the dance, right?" Jade began. Her friends nodded, and she continued, "So I thought

we could dress up
as pop stars, and
then actually *be* the
stars of the ball!"

"Jade, that's
perfect!" Yasmin
exclaimed.

"I can't believe I
didn't think of it
myself," Sasha
added, frowning.

"But how do we
snag that perfor-
mance spot?" Cloe
asked. "I mean, this
is a huge
event—I'm sure Mayor Davis has been audition-
ing bands for weeks already."

"Don't worry," Sasha said calmly. "The mayor
and I are pals. I'll get us the audition."

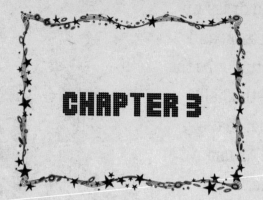

CHAPTER 3

I can't believe you just called up the mayor and got us the audition," Cloe told Sasha in amazement.

"Yeah, great job, Sash," Yasmin agreed. "Now we just need something to audition *with*."

The girls were lounging around Yasmin's bedroom — Cloe and Yasmin sprawled on the bed, Sasha perched on a butterfly chair, and Jade chilling on a couple of overstuffed cushions on the floor.

"Can't we use some of our Rock Angelz songs?" Cloe suggested. "I mean, everybody loved those."

"No way!" Jade cried. "We need a sound to go with our cool new look. Those outfits are totally not rock 'n' roll."

"True," Sasha agreed. "Besides, it'll be more fun to try out something new."

"But our audition's in a week, and we have absolutely nothing to perform," Cloe pointed out. "Don't you think that's sort of a problem?"

"We'll get there," Yasmin replied. "A few hours ago, we had no clue what to wear for the dance, and now we have fabulous new costumes. I'm sure we'll figure out our new sound, too."

"But making music isn't as easy as picking out clothes," Sasha told her.

"Hey!" Jade protested. "Coming up with a whole new look that works for all of us isn't exactly a piece of cake."

"I know, I know," Sasha said. "But it will take us more than a couple of hours to write all-new songs."

"Well, then, we better get practicing," Yasmin suggested, whipping out the notebook in which she jotted down all of her ideas, from short stories to song lyrics.

The girls all sat up straighter, ready to brainstorm. But a few hours later, they were all slumped back into their seats, defeated.

"Okay, what about this?" Sasha asked. She hummed a melody, and the girls shook their heads.

"Really cool, but don't you think it's a little edgy for a pop group?" Jade inquired.

"I guess," Sasha admitted.

"Ooh, I have something," Yasmin announced. She had been flipping through her notebook to find some song lyrics she'd been working on. She sang a few lines, and the girls sighed.

"That's really pretty, Yas, but it doesn't exactly scream 'pop sensation,'" Cloe pointed out.

"I know." Yasmin closed her notebook. "But that was the last thing I had."

"Okay, what if we pick our lead singer first," Sasha suggested, "and then we can come up with songs that are perfect for her?"

"That should be me," Jade declared, "because having a band was my idea and all."

"Or me," Cloe chimed in. "You girls know I love the spotlight."

"It should totally be me," Sasha protested. "I'm the one who's plugged into the music scene. If we need a new sound, I'm your girl."

They turned to Yasmin, who shrugged. "I don't care if I'm the lead singer. I just want to have fun with you girls."

"Aww, that's the spirit," Jade said. "Why can't you girls be like that?" she asked Cloe and Sasha.

"Just because you came up with the idea,

doesn't mean you get to run the whole show," Sasha complained.

"Why not?" Jade snapped. "That's usually what it means when *you* have an idea."

"That's so not true!" Sasha protested, leaping up from her chair.

"Girls, girls, settle down," Yasmin interrupted. "We're just frustrated because we don't know what to sing. So why don't we listen to some of our favorite tunes and get some musical ideas from them?"

"Good idea, Yas," Cloe chimed in, and the others nodded.

Yasmin hopped up to plug her iPod into her speaker system. She searched through her music collection, then chose an upbeat album she'd just bought. "I think you girls are going to love this!" she declared.

Yasmin bobbed her head to the music, but

Sasha complained, "This is, like, dance music. We need straight-up pop."

"But I think tunes with a beat are totally cool," Yasmin told her friend. "It adds an extra something, you know?"

"Well, let's see what else you have," Sasha suggested. She scrolled through Yasmin's playlist and chose a hip-hop jam. "Now this would be fun to perform!"

She started dancing, getting really into it, but Jade grabbed the iPod and chose a girl-power ballad instead. "Don't you girls think this is totally us?" she asked, hopping around in time to the peppy beat.

"Wait, listen to this," Cloe interjected. She flipped to the song that had been topping the charts for the past few weeks and closed her eyes, soaking it in.

"That's definitely pop music," Jade admitted. "But, I don't know —"

"It's just so bland!" Sasha interrupted. "How can we express ourselves with bubblegum pop like that?"

"But you said you *wanted* pop!" Cloe cried. "I don't get you girls. It's too upbeat, it's not upbeat enough, it's too distinctive, it's too bland. I can't figure out what you want." She turned off the music and added, "And I'm tired of trying. I just wanted to have fun at this year's Masquerade Ball, but all this bickering is totally ruining it for me." She turned on her heel and stormed out of the room, slamming the door behind her.

Her friends stared at each other in stunned silence. "She's right, you know," Yasmin said softly. "We're never going to get anywhere if we keep shooting each other down."

"That's true," Sasha agreed.

"It's just hard to agree on the right sound," Jade added.

"I know," Yasmin replied. "But we have to try." She got up and ran after Cloe, whom she found sitting on the back porch, her arms wrapped around her knees, her hair falling over her face.

"It's okay, Cloe," Yasmin whispered, putting her arms around her friend. "We're friends first, forever. Nothing can change that, ever. We'll get through this, like always, you'll see."

She looked up, and noticed that Sasha and Jade had followed her outside.

"Yasmin, that was beautiful," Sasha murmured. "In fact, I think we may have found our first song."

She started humming a melody, and Yasmin sang her comforting words, adapting them to fit Sasha's tune. The song was fun and cheerful, but still totally real, and soon Jade joined in, adding her own unique harmonies. Cloe finally looked up, and smiled, and started singing, too.

"That was incredible!" Jade exclaimed when the song was over.

"Yasmin, you should definitely sing lead on that one," Sasha announced. "I mean, it's really your song."

"If you want me to," Yasmin agreed.

"We do!" her friends chorused, making Yasmin grin.

"Then I think we should each take the lead on a few songs of our own," Yasmin suggested. "How's that sound?"

"Awesome!" the girls exclaimed.

"I'm glad we're all in agreement," Yasmin said with a smile. "But now we better get this song written down before we forget it!" The four best friends dashed inside, and Yasmin started scribbling lyrics while Sasha jotted down the musical line, with Jade and Cloe helping them both when they were unsure of what came next.

"We're on a roll!" Cloe declared. She got freaked

out easily, but she was easy to cheer up again, too.

"Just nine more songs to go," Sasha said.

"Oh, is that all?" Jade asked, making all of her friends laugh.

CHAPTER 4

A marathon songwriting sleepover was a fabulous idea," Cloe told Yasmin. It was Friday night, and they had tons of work to do for their audition. So the girls had all run home to grab their pajamas and guitars and to get their parents' permission to stay over at Yasmin's.

When they met back at her place, she greeted them with pizza and sodas. "I figured we needed to keep our energy up," she explained.

They gathered around Yasmin's kitchen table, the pizza boxes open in front of them, chatting as they eagerly grabbed slices with their favorite toppings. When they'd polished off the last piece, Sasha looked at the clock and gasped.

"We better get to work!" she exclaimed. "We've got a ton still to do."

"Do we really need ten songs for our audition?" Jade asked. "That seems like a lot."

"It *is* a lot," Sasha told her. "And no, we don't need all of them for the audition. But if we want to be able to play a couple of sets, like we'll have to if we get the gig, then yeah, we need ten songs."

"Okay, well, if we need that many, then I have an idea," Yasmin announced. "Why don't we all write songs in our fave style, like we were suggesting earlier, and then we'll all work on them together so that they fit into an overall sound."

"You know what?" Sasha replied. "I think that just might work!"

The girls camped out in Yasmin's room, each writing down lyrics or humming tunes to herself in her own corner of the room. Eventually Cloe hopped up and said, "Okay, listen to this!"

She sang a bouncy, peppy tune, and when she was finished, her friends cheered. "Cloe, that's exactly the sound I was imagining!" Jade cried.

"Well, I thought about what we were talking about and tried to match that sound," Cloe explained. "I'm glad you like it!"

"Who's up next?" Sasha asked.

"How about you?" Jade suggested.

Sasha shrugged and stood up. She sang a pop tune infused with a hip-hop groove, throwing in some dance moves to play up her song's rhythms. She struck a pose on the last note, and her friends applauded.

"That'll be so much fun to sing!" Yasmin declared.

"Let's hear what you came up with, Yasmin," Jade said.

Yasmin got up, looking shy. She started out

softly, but as she noticed her friends' encouraging expressions, she started singing louder, her voice getting clearer and stronger as the song went on. She had worked in a little bit of a salsa flavor to her pop music, and when she finished, her friends leaped up and wrapped her in a hug.

"I don't know what you were nervous about," Cloe told her. "That was totally dazzling!"

"I just—I wasn't sure it was what you were looking for," Yasmin said softly.

"It's exactly what we need!" Jade exclaimed. She smiled at her friends, proud of them for getting it together so quickly.

"Oh, right—you're waiting for me!" she exclaimed, noticing the girls watching her. She took her spot in the center of the room and launched into a driving tune all about girl power and doing your own thing.

When the song was over, Cloe cried, "Jade, you're a superstar!"

"I do what I can," Jade replied modestly. "I used our outfits for inspiration and tried to make my song sparkle just like those threads do."

"Well, it worked!" Yasmin told her.

"Girls, we're off to an awesome start!" Sasha announced. They gave each other high fives, then settled in to practice one another's songs.

"Oh my gosh, I don't think I can sing anymore," Cloe exclaimed after hours of practicing, writing more songs together, in pairs, and individually. She slumped onto the bed, draping her arm dramatically across her forehead. "I need a break!"

"How about a smoothie break?" Jade suggested. "They're tasty *and* good for your vocal cords!"

"Sounds good to me," Sasha agreed.

Yasmin followed Jade to the kitchen to help her mix up some banana-berry smoothies. "It's going really well, don't you think?" Yasmin asked, as Jade pressed the start button on the blender.

"After a rocky start, yeah, it's going well," Jade agreed. "I'm just glad we could pull it all together."

They each carried two smoothies back to Yasmin's room and passed them around.

"Girls, this audition is in the bag," Cloe declared. "I can feel it!"

"As long as we keep rehearsing," Sasha added. "In fact, as soon as we finish these smoothies, I think we should do a run-through of everything we have so far. Okay?"

"Okay," the girls replied, sounding sleepy.

"Sasha, maybe we should call it a night," Yasmin suggested when they had all finished their smoothies but couldn't seem to get up from their seats.

"We can get up early in the morning and keep going," Jade added, struggling to keep her eyes open. "But I think I'm all sung out for now."

"Me, too," Sasha admitted. "Cloe, are you as

beat as the rest of us?" She turned to her friend, who was curled up on Yasmin's bed, and that's when she noticed that Cloe had already fallen asleep!

"Guess that's a 'yes,'" Jade pointed out, laughing.

"I don't think we can move her, Yas," Sasha said.

"It's okay," Yasmin replied. "She's just taking up a little corner—I can sleep on the other side." Jade and Sasha unrolled their sleeping bags on the floor, and within moments, they were all fast asleep, without any of the late-night chatter that usually followed lights-out at their sleepovers. They were just too tired to say another word.

* * *

Sasha was up first the next morning, as usual, and carried in a tray of orange juice, muffins, and fruit that Yasmin's mom had told her they could have for breakfast.

"Rise and shine!" Sasha called. Her friends wiped groggily at their eyes, sitting up slowly. "I have muffins!" she added, and the girls got up faster.

"Mmm, cranberry!" Jade exclaimed, grabbing a muffin and biting into it. "These always give me energy!"

The girls happily ate their breakfast, and then Sasha announced, "Okay, back to work! Let's see if everyone remembers what we practiced last night!"

They ran through all five songs they had written the night before, pausing to change lyrics or guitar chords or to add in a dance move.

"I think these songs are totally ready!" Jade declared.

"We'll have to keep practicing, though," Sasha warned.

"Of course," Jade agreed. "But still, we're halfway there! Not bad for one night."

"At this rate, we'll be all set by the time the weekend's over!" Cloe exclaimed.

The girls practiced all day on Saturday and got permission to sleep over at Yasmin's again that night so they could keep practicing on Sunday. By Monday, they were all sung out, but they also had a full set ready for the Masquerade Ball!

"Mayor Davis won't believe her ears," Jade announced on the drive to school Monday morning.

"Yeah, when she hears us, she'll just send all the other bands home!" Cloe predicted.

"I'm sure the other groups will be great, too," Yasmin said. "But we'll be better!" The girls cheered, their cries floating out the open windows as the wind whipped through their long hair. At that moment, none of the girls could imagine feeling happier or more excited than they were right then.

CHAPTER 5

After school every day that week, the girls met to do their homework, followed by as much practicing as they could fit in. By the time Saturday rolled around, they were totally pumped for their audition.

They arrived at the town hall early that morning in their cute new outfits, their guitars slung over their shoulders as they sipped hot green tea to help them wake up. But when they walked into the main lobby, they were startled to see ten other bands all lined up to perform, too.

"I thought this was a private audition," Jade whispered to Sasha.

"Well, I guess the mayor just wants to keep her options open," Sasha replied.

"Oh my gosh, there's Meygan!" Cloe squealed, spotting her redheaded friend among the musicians. "And Fianna and Vinessa are with her too!" She rushed over to say hi, and Jade, Sasha, and Yasmin followed her.

"I didn't know you girls were trying out, too!" Meygan exclaimed, hugging her friends. Fianna and Vinessa joined in, and soon they were in one big huddle.

"Uh-oh, we're in for some serious competition," Fianna said with a laugh.

"I know, maybe we shouldn't be associating with the enemy," Jade teased.

"We're not really up against each other!" Vinessa pointed out. "Mayor Davis is looking for two acts for the evening—so we'll just have to snag both spots!"

As if responding to her name, Mayor Davis strode out of her office and clapped her hands to get everyone's attention. The room went silent immediately as everyone turned to listen to her announcements. "First, I want to thank all of you for coming. I'm excited to have live music for the first time at this year's Masquerade Ball, and I'm thrilled that so many of you wanted to help make that happen."

The bands applauded, and the mayor paused, smiling, until they quieted down again. "I'll have each group come into my office to perform, and I'll announce my selections once everyone has auditioned, so I suggest that you all stick around until the end. The whole process shouldn't require more than two hours of your time."

She glanced at the list in her hand and called

Meygan's band, the Red Hearts, into her office. Since Meygan had formed the band, they'd decided to name themselves after her flame-red hair.

Cloe, Jade, Sasha, and Yasmin wished their friends luck, but as soon as the door to Mayor Davis's office closed, they exchanged worried glances. They headed to a corner of the lobby, away from the other groups, so they could strategize. All four girls sat cross-legged on the marble floor and talked in hushed voices so they wouldn't be overheard.

"There's no way she'll pick two girl bands," Sasha told them. "She wants two bands to give the dance some variety, you know?"

"Well then, let's hope we're better than them," Jade said with a shrug.

"Jade! Those are our friends!" Cloe protested.

"Yeah, but if it's us or them, we need it to be us," Jade pointed out. "Because if we don't get this slot, we're going to have to find new costumes. It would be way too embarrassing to go as music stars if we weren't even picked to perform."

"That's true," Yasmin agreed. "But I think we have a more pressing problem."

"Oh no, what?" Cloe cried. "I can't deal with another problem!"

"It's not huge," Yasmin began, "but it is important. We need a name for our band."

"I can't believe I didn't think of that!" Sasha exclaimed. "I must be losing my planning touch."

"Well, we were kind of busy, what with writing and rehearsing ten songs in the last week," Jade reminded her. "You can see how it might have slipped our minds."

"It's up to you, Yasmin," Sasha announced. "You're our 'words' girl."

"Hmm . . ." Yasmin looked up toward the ceiling as though searching for inspiration.

"Pick something that makes us sound like real stars!" Cloe added.

Yasmin turned to Cloe excitedly, snapped out of her thoughts by her friend's outburst. "Cloe, you're a genius!"

"Well, *I* always thought so," Cloe replied, twirling her blonde hair around her finger and trying to look modest. "But tell me why *you* think so."

"We should call ourselves the Stars!" Yasmin announced.

"No, the Starz, with a 'z,'" Jade suggested. "It's hipper, you know?"

"Totally," Sasha agreed. "But why not go one step further and call ourselves the Super Starz?"

"Perfect!" Cloe cried. "Awesome quick thinking, ladies!"

"I knew we could do it," Yasmin said. "We always come up with the best ideas when we all work together."

Meygan, Fianna, and Vinessa emerged from the mayor's office and hurried over to join their friends, while a girl who was singing solo headed in for her audition. The Super Starz scooted back to let the other girls grab spots in a circle on the floor.

"So, how was it?" Sasha asked the Red Hearts.

"I think it went really well," Meygan replied. "Mayor Davis is totally cool, so she really put us at ease."

"We sang three songs, and she seemed to be into all of them," Fianna added.

"That's great," Cloe told them. "I really hope all of us get to perform at the dance!"

"Love your outfits," Jade added, checking out the girls' jewel-toned tank tops with metallic details, paired with boot-cut jeans and open-toed high heels. "You all look utterly glam!"

"Thanks," Meygan said. "We found them at Fashion Friendz-y, at the mall."

"No way!" Cloe cried. "We couldn't find *any-thing* when we were there last week!"

"Well, we got them a few weeks ago," Vinessa explained. "We wanted to make sure we had our look together way in advance so we could concentrate on rehearsals instead."

"Makes sense," Sasha replied, shooting quick glances at the rest of her band. The Red Hearts had been practicing for way longer than they had!

The soloist emerged from the office, and a boy band went in.

Vinessa offered to grab them all some snacks and headed to the coffee shop across the street. By the time she got back, it was time for the Super Starz to audition. "We'll grab a cookie afterward," Jade said as they headed into the mayor's office.

"Good to see you all again," Mayor Davis greeted them as they set up their instruments. "Well, let's get started."

The girls opened with Yasmin's song, the first one they'd written, and it went perfectly. They were excited to see Mayor Davis bobbing her head along with the music.

Encouraged, they launched into the next song, with Cloe in the lead. She didn't miss a beat, but Jade got mixed up on a few words, which threw off Sasha and Yasmin, and soon all three backup singers were singing the wrong lines. Cloe sang louder to drown them out, hoping the mayor wouldn't notice, and her friends quickly got back on track. This was one of the first songs they'd written, and they'd been in such a hurry to work on all the later songs that they clearly hadn't practiced this one enough.

Sasha was nervous as she stepped up to sing one of her songs, afraid that they'd already blown the audition. This time, everyone remembered all the words. But halfway through, Cloe forgot her dance moves and stood still for a moment. She saw her friends doing a twirl out of the corner of her eye and quickly did the same — but her timing was off and she crashed into Yasmin, who had already started doing her next move.

Both girls grabbed at each other to keep from falling, then picked up the next part of the routine. At the end of the song, all four girls struck a pose with their hands on their hips, trying to smile, but they were sure that their mistakes had ruined their chances of getting the gig.

"Great sound, girls," Mayor Davis said. "I think you have some more work to do, but overall, I enjoyed it."

"Thank you," they murmured, and shuffled back into the lobby with their heads down.

"What happened?" Fianna asked when she saw them looking completely bummed out.

"I messed up the words," Jade admitted.

"And I forgot our dance moves, and almost crushed Yasmin!" Cloe added.

"There's no way we're getting that spot," Yasmin said sadly.

"I knew we should've practiced more!" Sasha cried.

"Sash, we used every spare moment for rehearsals," Jade reminded her. "What more could we have done—practiced in our sleep?"

"If that's what it took," Sasha replied.

"I'm sure you were fine," Vinessa said soothingly, but her friends shook their heads.

"I don't think so," Cloe told her. "But I hope you girls get a spot, anyway! We'll definitely be there to cheer you on."

The girls munched on the cookies that Vinessa had brought them while the next few acts auditioned for the mayor. The Red Hearts kept trying to cheer up their friends, but the Super Starz were too upset to talk much.

Soon, the last audition was over, and the mayor reappeared in the lobby to announce her decision.

"You all did a great job," she began, "but as you know, I can only choose two bands. It wasn't an easy choice, but after careful consideration, I've decided that our performers for this year's Masquerade Ball will be the Red Hearts and the Super Starz!"

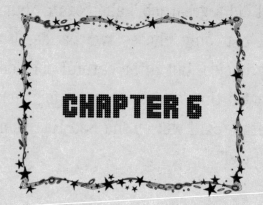

CHAPTER 6

The seven friends squealed, jumping up and down and hugging each other excitedly.

"I can't believe it!" Cloe exclaimed.

"I knew you could do it," Vinessa told her friends.

"I'm glad *you* did," Sasha replied. "Because I wasn't quite sure."

"I'm looking forward to seeing everyone at the dance next week!" Mayor Davis called as the other bands packed up and headed out of the town hall.

The two bands she'd picked were walking out together when the mayor stopped the Super Starz.

"Can I have a word with you girls?" she asked.

They exchanged worried glances, but Sasha said brightly, "Sure! No problem!" Turning to Meygan, Fianna, and Vinessa, she added, "We'll catch up with you guys later."

When the Red Hearts had cleared out, Mayor Davis said seriously, "I think you girls have a lot of potential, but you know you have a lot of work to do before the dance, right?"

The girls hung their heads, embarrassed, but she continued, "I know you can do this. I wouldn't have chosen you if I didn't think you could handle it. But this is Stilesville's biggest event of the year, so I need you to really polish all ten songs you'll be performing at the ball. Can you do that?"

"Yes, Mayor Davis," they promised.

"We won't let you down!" Cloe cried.

"Good. I'll let you get back to practicing, then." Mayor Davis gave them a wave, and the girls gathered up their equipment and headed outside.

"I can't believe we got it," Yasmin murmured as they walked toward their cars.

"We better get to work," Sasha declared. "We can't mess up like that at the dance — we'll never live it down!"

"We won't," Jade insisted.

"Not if we keep practicing," Sasha agreed.

The girls hurried back to Sasha's place to rehearse. She had microphones and speakers set up in her garage, so they could practice with the equipment they'd have on the night of the dance.

"Okay, let's run all the dance routines, then all the songs, and then we'll try them all together again," Sasha said.

"Shouldn't we just run through the songs the way we'll be performing them?" Jade asked. "I mean, we'll be here forever if we divide it all up like that."

"We tried practicing it all together before," Sasha reminded her, "and you saw how well that worked out."

"Hey, we got the gig, didn't we?" Jade pointed out. She crossed her arms over her chest and narrowed her eyes at Sasha.

"Yeah, barely," Sasha snapped. "We don't want Mayor Davis to regret giving us a chance, do we?"

"Of course not," Jade admitted. "But we'll do an awesome job, I'm sure of it!"

"You could've fooled me," Sasha muttered.

"What?" Jade demanded.

"Look, you forgot the words, and that's fine, it happens," Sasha replied. "But I need you to help me out if we're going to be ready to perform in a week."

"Help *you* out?" Jade cried. "I'm sorry, I thought this band was *my* idea."

"Sure it was," Sasha agreed. "But now we need my leadership if we're going to whip this band into shape."

Yasmin looked from Sasha to Jade worriedly. She hated to see her friends fighting like this. "I'm sure we'll be ready in time if we all work together," Yasmin suggested.

"We clearly need some leadership," Sasha insisted. "And I'm the girl for the job."

"You know what, Sasha?" Jade shouted. "I'm tired of you bossing us around! And I don't know what you're freaking out about, anyway — we're doing fine so far!"

"See, that's your problem," Sasha told her. "You think everything will just work out on its own, but it won't. And that's exactly why I have to take charge."

"Well, you have fun with that," Jade replied. "In the meantime, I'm going to go see if Meygan's band needs another member." With that, she stalked off, and her friends stared after her, stunned.

"Sasha, you have to stop her," Cloe cried. "We can't go on without Jade!"

"I didn't do anything," Sasha said with a shrug. "I wouldn't know what to apologize for."

"You were kind of harsh," Yasmin chimed in. "I know Jade felt terrible about forgetting the words, but the rest of us messed up, too. We were probably just tired from all that rehearsing."

"Oh, so now you're turning on me too?" Sasha demanded.

"No!" Yasmin strode over to Sasha and put a hand on her friend's arm comfortingly. "You know we love your take-charge attitude, but maybe you overdid it just a little this time."

"Do you think I went too far?" Sasha asked, turning to Cloe.

Cloe looked down at her boots, scuffing the toes of her shoes against the concrete floor, but finally she murmured, "Yeah. You kind of did."

"But I know how important the Masquerade Ball is to all of you!" Sasha cried. "I just want things to go perfectly, for all our sakes!"

"We know, Sasha," Yasmin told her. "But you know what? I think Jade wants everything to go perfectly, too, and it can't have felt good to know that you didn't think she was up for the job."

"I never said that!" Sasha protested. "Jade knows I think she's amazing." But when she saw her friends shaking their heads, she added, "Doesn't she?"

"Right now, I'm not sure if she does," Cloe said softly.

Sasha took in her friends' concerned expressions, then nodded determinedly. "Okay. I'll go get her back."

"That's our Sasha!" Cloe exclaimed as Sasha dashed out of the garage, clearly a girl on a mission.

CHAPTER 7

Sasha drove over to Jade's house. But when she saw that her friend wasn't home, she figured she'd try Jade's home away from home—the Stilesville Mall. She couldn't think of anywhere else her friend would have gone when she was this upset.

Sasha spotted Jade's car in the mall parking lot and parked next to her, relieved that her hunch had been right. She power-walked through the mall, peering into all of their favorite stores, but she didn't see Jade anywhere. She stopped off at the food court to grab a bottle of water, and that was when she spotted Jade at a table with Meygan.

Sasha ducked behind a huge potted plant so Jade wouldn't see her. She knew she wasn't exactly Jade's favorite person at the moment.

"I just don't think I can take it anymore," Sasha heard Jade explaining to Meygan.

"That sounds rough," Meygan agreed. "But you know Sasha means well, right?"

"Sure," Jade admitted. "But she has to learn that she can't just push people around all the time!"

"It isn't fun to be pushed around—but isn't it nice sometimes to have someone who will really push you, beyond what even you thought you could do?" Meygan asked.

"I guess . . ." Jade stared off at the other tables at the food court, packed with laughing, chattering shoppers. "But sometimes it's just too much."

"I totally understand," Meygan said sympathetically. "I wish there was something I could do to help."

"Actually, there is," Jade replied. She took a deep breath and then let her words pour out in a rush, before she could stop herself. "I really don't think I can play with my band anymore. Not after what Sasha said to me. So I was wondering if I could maybe join yours."

From her spot behind the plant, Sasha gasped and clapped her hand over her mouth to stifle the sound. She'd never really thought Jade would leave the band—she'd figured her friend just needed some time to cool down and then she'd be back at practice and everything would be back to normal.

"Of course you can, if that's what you want," Meygan told Jade. "I hate to see you girls fighting, though. Isn't there any chance you and Sasha will make up?"

"I'm sure we will eventually," Jade admitted. "I mean, we've been best friends, like, forever."

"Then why not do it now?" Meygan suggested. "Then you can perform with the Super Starz like you'd planned, instead of having to learn a whole new batch of songs with us."

"That *would* be a lot of work," Jade admitted. "But I'm willing to do it, if that's what it takes!"

"But you don't have to," Meygan insisted. "I'm sure Sasha feels bad about what happened and that she'll be as eager to make up as you are."

"You really think so?" Jade asked hopefully. "That would be great. I mean, it'd be fun to perform with you girls, but it would be weird to see Cloe, Sasha, and Yasmin go onstage without me. And I worked on a lot of songs with them that I'd hate to see go to waste."

Sasha, encouraged by Jade's words, leaped out of her hiding place. Jade and Meygan jumped back from their table, startled to discover that their friend had been crouching right beside their table. "Jade, I'm so glad you want to make up!" she cried.

"Sasha, what are you doing?" Jade shouted.

"Well, I saw you guys sitting there talking, and I didn't want to bother you, so—" Sasha began, but Jade cut her off.

"So you spied on us? That's a great idea," Jade snapped. "You are just *full* of great ideas today, Sasha." Jade stood up quickly and shoved her chair back under the table, her movements brisk and angry. "I can't believe I was about to forgive you."

"Jade, I'm sorry, I—" Sasha began, but Jade wouldn't listen.

"It's not cool to order your friends around," Jade told her. "And it's not cool to spy on them, either."

"I know, that was wrong of me, it's just—" Sasha continued. But Jade was already storming out of the food court, her glossy black hair bouncing against her back as she hurried away. "It's just that I didn't know what to say to get you to come back," she finished softly.

Sasha turned to Meygan, who still sat at the table she and Jade had shared, her chin resting on her hands as she watched the drama unfold.

"I think that went well," Sasha said wryly.

"It could have gone better," Meygan agreed. Sasha slumped into the chair across from Meygan, looking defeated. "Look," Meygan continued, "you know she'll get over it. It's just a question of when."

"Yeah, and what I'll have to do to convince her I'm not completely out of my mind," Sasha added.

"Well, hiding in the shrubbery *is* a little crazy," Meygan pointed out. "You can see why she would be a bit shocked."

"I know," Sasha admitted. "I just don't think

our band can manage without her. I was trying to do whatever it takes to win her back."

"So what do you want me to do?" Meygan asked. "Refuse to let her join our band?"

"No!" Sasha cried. "She's at least as excited about performing at the ball as I am—she can't miss out on that. If she really doesn't feel like she can be a part of our band anymore, then she has to join yours. And I'm sure you could use another great singer, right?"

"Totally," Meygan replied. "And Sasha?" Sasha finally met Meygan's gaze and saw the concern and caring in her friend's deep blue eyes. "That was the answer of a true friend."

"Thanks," Sasha said softly.

"Jade knows what a good friend you are, too," Meygan added. "She's hurt right now, but I know she'll come around."

"I hope you're right." Sasha stood up from the

table and trudged back to her car, then drove slowly back to her house, dreading going back to her garage and telling her friends that she'd upset Jade once again, that Jade wouldn't be rejoining their band anytime soon.

CHAPTER 8

"Welcome to your very first Red Hearts rehearsal!" Fianna exclaimed when Jade arrived at Meygan's place that night.

"Thanks for having me," Jade replied. "I hope I'm not intruding."

"Of course you aren't!" Meygan told her. "I mean, four cool girls has got to be better than three, right?"

"Makes sense to me," Jade agreed. She strolled into Meygan's front room and sat cross-legged on a cushy blue chair. "So, where do we start?"

"Why don't we perform our whole set for you, and then you can start learning your part?" Vinessa suggested.

"Perfect!" Jade said. "I'll just sit back and enjoy the show."

Her three friends started singing and dancing, and Jade watched carefully, so when it was her turn to try, she already knew some of the words and dance moves. The girls were thrilled to see how quickly Jade was picking up their routine — and they were sure their act would be even better now that they were a foursome!

But over at Sasha's house, things weren't going nearly as well. The girls were trying to rework their songs, but they just kept falling flat without Jade's part.

"We can't do it without Jade," Cloe cried, collapsing dramatically in the middle of Sasha's bedroom floor. "Sasha, you have to get her to come back. Our act is hopeless without her."

"Come on, Cloe, get up," Sasha said, reaching for her friend.

But Cloe pulled away, insisting, "You have to *do* something. We can't go on like this."

"I tried, okay?" Sasha told her. "And I failed. If you think you can do better, why don't you go over there?"

"Maybe I will," Cloe replied. She hopped up and ran out of the room.

"Great, we lost another one," Sasha said.

"Don't worry, she'll be back," Yasmin told her. "Come on, let's grab some dinner while we wait for her."

"Okay," Sasha agreed. "But we do have a lot of rehearsing to do."

"I know." Yasmin guided Sasha toward the kitchen so they could forage for food, and added, "When Cloe gets back, we'll practice all night long if we have to."

* * *

Cloe burst into Meygan's living room in time to see the four Red Hearts wrapping up their set.

"Hey, what's up, Cloe?" Fianna asked.

"Jade, can I talk to you for just a sec?" Cloe motioned to her best friend to follow her onto the front porch.

Jade looked at her bandmates to see if it was okay. "Can we take a little break?"

"Of course!" Meygan replied. "Take as long as you need. We'll just be chilling in here."

On the porch, Cloe pulled a small gold box out of her slouchy white shoulder bag and handed it to Jade.

"What's this?" Jade wanted to know.

"Just a little something that I thought would look perfect with your costume," Cloe said.

"But you know I'm probably going to wear something else to perform with the Red Hearts," Jade pointed out.

"Jade, you can't!" Cloe cried. "You love that

outfit you picked out with us. I mean, you designed our band's whole look."

"I know," Jade replied, "but this is what I have to do."

"You do not!" Cloe insisted. "Come back to our band. Things will be better, you'll see. Sasha is really sorry, and you know Yasmin and I want you back, and—"

"Cloe, things are going really well with the Red Hearts," Jade interrupted. "I'm not going to ditch them now, okay?"

Cloe leaned against the porch railing with a sigh. "Okay. But will you at least open the box?"

"I can do that," Jade agreed. She pulled the lid off the box and smiled when she saw the shiny gold bangles that Cloe had nestled inside. "They're gorgeous!" Jade exclaimed.

"I know they'll look great onstage," Cloe told her. "Even if you won't go onstage with us, you have to wear them, okay?"

"I can do that," Jade agreed. "I'm sure they'll look fabulous with whatever outfit I find to wear with the Red Hearts."

"I'm sure they will," Cloe replied, giving her friend a quick hug. "I'm so glad you liked them."

"Well, I better get back to rehearsing," Jade said.

"Yeah, me too." Cloe hurried toward her car, waving over her shoulder as she went.

Jade watched her best friend's car pull away, then strolled back inside to resume practicing with her new band.

Cloe screeched down the road to Sasha's place, tires squealing as she jerked to a stop in front of the house. She jumped out of her car and stomped up to the front door, throwing it open so it slammed against the wall.

"Whoa, Cloe, take it easy on the house, there," Sasha said from her spot on the couch. She and Yasmin sat side by side, eating thick sandwiches they'd assembled for dinner.

"I hope you're happy," Cloe hissed at Sasha. "Jade is staying with the Red Hearts, and I'm starting to think that maybe I should follow her."

"Hey, what happened?" Yasmin asked worriedly. She set her sandwich on her plate on the coffee table and got up to comfort her friend.

As Yasmin pulled her into a hug, Cloe murmured, "I really thought I could convince Jade to come back, you know? But now I know it's hopeless."

"No it isn't," Yasmin told her. "We'll get her back, okay? I promise." Cloe's blue eyes glistened with tears as she looked hopefully at Yasmin, and Yasmin only hoped that was a promise she could keep.

CHAPTER 9

Yasmin ducked into the bathroom and speed-dialed Fianna, who she knew was in charge of organizing the Red Hearts' rehearsals. "Okay, are you as sick of all this fighting as I am?" Yasmin whispered into the phone.

"Of course I am," Fianna replied. "It's awful seeing such good friends bickering. Plus, it's kind of interfering with our rehearsals."

"Ours, too," Yasmin agreed. "But I have a plan to fix it, and I need your help."

The next day, both bands arrived at the fancy

Stilesville Centre Hotel, the site of the Masquerade Ball, ready to rehearse on the stage where they'd be performing that Saturday.

"Wow, it's gorgeous in here," Vinessa murmured, taking in the marble columns and crystal chandeliers. Vinessa was new in town, and this would be her first Masquerade Ball.

"I know, I love this place," Jade replied. Then she turned and saw her former bandmates entering the lobby. "Hey, what're they doing here?" she demanded.

"Oh, hey girls," Fianna called. "Sorry, did we get our times mixed up?"

"Looks like we double-booked the stage," Yasmin said. "I guess we'll just have to share our rehearsal time."

"So this wasn't an elaborate scheme to get Jade and me in the same room again?" Sasha asked.

"Maybe it was, and maybe it wasn't," Fianna replied.

"You aren't mad, are you?" Yasmin looked anxious, but determined. "We didn't want to trick you, but it was the only way we could think of to get you two together."

"It was underhanded, and sneaky, and—and a really good idea." Jade walked over to Sasha and smiled slightly. "Look, I'm tired of fighting. What do you say we give in to their little scheme?"

"I'd be happy to," Sasha replied, throwing her arms around Jade. The two girls hugged for a long moment, both murmuring apologies. When they stepped back, their friends all cheered, thrilled that everything was back to normal at last.

"One question, though," Meygan began. "Now that you two have made up, which band is Jade performing with, anyway?"

"Oh," Jade said softly. "I don't know. I mean, I worked so hard with the Super Starz, but I don't want to abandon the Red Hearts, either."

Turning to Meygan, Fianna, and Vinessa, she

continued, "It was so sweet of you girls to let me join your band at the last minute. I can't tell you how much that meant to me."

"We were thrilled to have you," Vinessa told her, "but we'd understand if you want to go back to the Super Starz."

"But I do love our new sound now that you've joined up," Fianna added. "We'd definitely miss having you perform with us."

"I don't know what to do!" Jade cried. "I want to perform with both of you, but there's no way I can."

"Actually," Cloe interrupted, "I think there just might be."

The girls all looked at Cloe, eager to hear her plan. "What if we form one big band?" she suggested. "Then we can all hang out together all night, plus we'll all get more stage time. And best of all, Jade won't have to choose between us!"

"Do you think we'd all fit on the stage?" Fianna wondered.

"Sure we would!" Meygan said, gesturing toward the massive mahogany stage in front of them. "It's huge!"

"Having that many people all playing together would let us add all sorts of extra harmonies to our songs," Sasha pointed out. "It could give us a really incredible sound."

"Well, let's give it a try," Jade agreed. The girls all hopped onstage, and soon both groups were playing each other's songs.

"We sound amazing!" Cloe exclaimed. "I don't know why we didn't think of this sooner!"

"Um, guys?" Yasmin asked. "Don't you think we'd better make sure Mayor Davis is okay with the two groups she picked merging into just one?"

"I'm sure it'll be fine," Sasha assured her. But she called the mayor anyway, motioning for her friends to keep quiet while the phone rang.

When Mayor Davis picked up, Sasha explained the situation, and the mayor said it was fine with her if the girls didn't mind spending the whole ball onstage. She had picked two acts to make sure both groups would have some time on the dance floor, too. But Sasha assured her that since they would all be onstage together, she and her friends would have way more fun performing than they could have hanging out in the crowd.

"We're all set!" Sasha declared after she hung up the phone.

"Yay!" her friends all cheered.

"So should we combine our band names, or come up with something totally new?" Sasha asked.

"You know what?" Meygan replied. "I think the Super Starz is a totally cute name. I think we should all use it, if you original Starz are okay with that."

"That's awesome, Meygan," Yasmin said. "But are you sure you're okay with giving up your band's name? It's totally cute, too."

"Not a problem," Meygan told her. "But now, we better get down to business."

First, the girls divided up their instrumental parts. They decided that Meygan would take lead vocals, while Cloe, Sasha, and Yasmin played guitar. Jade would back them up on the bass, Fianna would play the drums, and Vinessa would handle the keyboard. Of course, they would each take the lead on certain songs and would switch instruments accordingly. Luckily, all seven girls knew how to play all of the instruments they would need onstage, so they had tons of flexibility.

"We're going to be the most spectacular girl band ever!" Cloe declared.

"Or at least the biggest," Jade replied, grinning.

Sasha helped her friends figure out new parts on their instruments now that they had so many to work with. She came up with some dance moves that would look amazing with seven girls doing them in sync, and her friends enthusiastically practiced their parts, twirling and dipping and jumping across the stage.

"Sasha, you're a totally talented choreographer!" Fianna exclaimed.

"*And* an awesome musician," Jade added. "In fact, I don't know what we'd do without her."

Sasha was beaming at her friends, but she just kept dancing, loving the feeling of being swept up in the rhythm and the movement and of being surrounded by her very best friends.

CHAPTER 10

The girls couldn't believe the night of the Masquerade Ball had finally arrived! They all planned to meet at Cloe's place to get dressed and to do each other's hair and makeup. The former Red Hearts hadn't shown up yet, but the Super Starz decided to start getting ready anyway.

"That way we'll have more time to help them when they get here," Jade pointed out.

The four best friends decided to wear their hair long and loose for a totally glam look. They paired up to give each other makeovers, sitting cross-legged across from each other on the floor of Cloe's bedroom. Jade gave Cloe pale pink eyeshadow and bright rose lipstick, and Cloe used the same lipstick for Jade, paired with a purple eyeshadow. Sasha brushed a light lilac shade on Yasmin's lids, then added bright pink lipstick, while Yasmin picked a shimmery brown eyeshadow for Sasha, along with lipstick in burgundy.

"Well, do I look like a pop star?" Sasha asked, striking a pose.

"We all do!" Cloe declared. "But where are our fellow pop stars? They better get here soon or they won't have any time to get ready."

"I'm sure they're on their way," Yasmin assured her.

But it wasn't until Cloe was knotting her skinny scarf, Jade was looping her long beaded necklace around her neck, Yasmin was positioning her floppy hat at a slight angle on her head, and Sasha was slipping into her shrug that Meygan and Fianna rushed through the door, already in costume and looking upset.

"What's wrong, you guys?" Yasmin asked.

"Vinessa's sick!" Fianna cried. "She just called and told us she can't go on tonight. She sounded so awful, and I feel terrible leaving her all by herself at home while we go out and have a blast."

"Poor 'Nessa!" Cloe exclaimed. "I can't believe she's missing the biggest event of the year."

"Well, if Vinessa can't come to the party, then we'll just have to bring the party to her," Sasha announced.

"What do you mean?" Meygan wanted to know.

"We're all ready to go early, so why don't we stop by Vinessa's house and give her a mini-concert right now?" Sasha suggested. "It'll be a great warm-up for us, and I bet it'll cheer her up, too."

"Great idea, Sasha!" Cloe exclaimed. "Come on, you guys, what are you waiting for?" She hustled her friends out the door, and they climbed into two cars for the ride over to Vinessa's.

During the car ride, Sasha made some quick notes on her clipboard. "Okay, Yasmin, you'll need to take keyboards, and Meygan can double on guitar. Then we should be all covered. Sound good?"

"Sounds great," Yasmin agreed. "Good thinking, Sash!"

They pulled up to Vinessa's house and knocked softly on the door, not wanting to disturb their friend if she was sleeping. Vinessa's mom answered the door, looking surprised to see six girls decked out in pop-star outfits on her porch. They explained their plan, and she agreed to let them in to play just a few songs before Vinessa went to sleep.

All six girls filed into Vinessa's room, instruments in hand, and formed a half-circle around her bed.

"Wha—what are you all doing here?" Vinessa asked groggily. Her nose was red and her eyes were watery—she had definitely come down with a bad cold.

"We thought a little music might make you feel better," Meygan explained. The girls started playing, and Vinessa's eyes lit up.

When they were finished, Vinessa clapped as hard as she could. "I'm so sorry I let you girls down," she said, "but you sound incredible without me, so I don't feel quite as bad!"

"Hey, it's not your fault you're sick," Jade told her. "Don't worry about us. We're just bummed that you're missing your very first Stilesville Masquerade Ball."

"There's always next year," Vinessa said in a hoarse, scratchy voice.

"Oh boy, we better let you rest up," Fianna declared. "You get better, okay?"

"Okay," Vinessa agreed.

Sasha glanced at her watch. "Uh-oh, we better get going. We're on in fifteen minutes!" The girls quickly packed up their instruments and loaded up their cars, then hurried over to the Stilesville Centre Hotel.

"Ooh, look at it," Yasmin sighed. Twinkling white lights were draped from every tree branch and bush and wrapped around every column on the front of the hotel so that the entire place seemed to sparkle.

"Totally magical," Fianna agreed.

"No," Jade corrected her, "once we take the stage, it'll be totally magical."

"Well then, we better get in there," Meygan replied. "Because I think Stilesville is ready for an enchanted evening!"

The six friends waded through the crowd, thrilled to see that the room was completely packed, and reached the stage just as Mayor Davis welcomed everyone to the annual Stilesville Masquerade Ball. The girls applauded along with the rest of the audience, and then the mayor announced, "And now, we have something really special for you. Put on your dancing shoes, because the Super Starz are ready to take the stage!"

The girls ran onstage with the crowd cheering them on. "Happy Halloween, everybody!" Meygan called into the microphone, and then she started to sing with five of her best friends backing her up.

As the girls looked past the bright spotlights that shone down on the stage, they noticed the lush orange, red, and yellow banners that swooped down from the ceiling, giving the ballroom a rich autumn harvest feel. They smiled at all the ghosts, witches, vampires, princesses, angels, and cats, all getting down together on the dance floor. And all six girls felt certain that this was the best Masquerade Ball that Stilesville had ever seen.

CHAPTER 11

Although the girls had agreed that they'd have
way more fun onstage than off, as the
evening wore on, they decided that they should
each take a turn on the dance floor, too, just to
get the full experience of the ball.

"One of the benefits of having such a big band,"
Sasha pointed out. She went first, and was immediately mobbed by all her friends, congratulating
her on their awesome tunes.

"Love the new sound, Sasha," her friend Dylan

exclaimed. "Let me know if you ever need a boy to join the band, okay?"

"Will do," Sasha promised, making her way to the dance floor, where her friend Felicia stopped her.

"Those dance moves were totally hot," Felicia said. "Do you think you could teach me a few?"

"Sure!" Sasha agreed. Soon they were both grooving to the music, and the crowd cleared a circle around them to watch their dazzling dance moves.

Sasha was so into it that at first she didn't notice her friends gesturing to her from the stage. "Uh-oh, my band needs me," she said.

"Okay, but you'll have to show me some more moves later," Felicia replied, and Sasha promised that she would.

Jade took her turn on the dance floor, and soon everyone was rushing over to ask her where she'd found their amazing costumes. She modestly explained that she'd just pieced them together at the mall.

"You have an incredible eye for fashion," her friend Dana told her. "The boots, the skirt — it's all working for you, girl!"

"I just hope the judges for the Best Costume award think so, too," Jade said.

"Oh come on, you know that prize is yours," her friend Nevra chimed in, joining the others by the punch bowl. She handed Jade a glass of strawberry punch, and Jade gulped it down, parched from all the singing.

Then Jade spotted Cloe hurrying through the crowd and waved good-bye to Dana and Nevra. "I better get back onstage," she explained.

On her way to the stage, she noticed Cloe talking to their friend Cameron and had to smile. Their friends were all sure that Cloe and Cameron had a thing for each other, but they always insisted they were just friends. Still, when she reached the stage, Jade whispered to her friends that maybe it was time for a slow song.

They started playing, and out in the audience Cameron looked shyly at Cloe. "Would you like to dance?" he asked.

"Okay," Cloe said softly. She was usually a big talker, but around Cameron she always seemed to be at a loss for words. When the song ended, she said, "Happy Halloween, Cameron," and then hurried back to the stage, where her friends were all shaking their heads and giggling at her.

"What?" she demanded. "What's so funny?" But none of her friends would answer her.

When Yasmin took her break, she headed straight for the snack table. She'd had her eye on a cupcake with orange frosting and white sprinkles all night long. As she bit into it, her friend Phoebe joined her, grabbing a cupcake of her own.

"Those are some super-sweet lyrics you girls have been singing tonight," Phoebe said. "Did you write them all yourself?"

"Oh, no, we all worked on them together," Yasmin explained. "Everything about this band was a team effort!"

"Well, it really paid off," Phoebe told her. "Everyone's saying they don't want to come to the ball next year unless you guys are playing!"

"Then I guess we'll just have to play again," Yasmin replied happily.

While Meygan and Fianna headed into the crowd to hang out with their friends Sienna and Maribel, the four original Super Starz played the first song they'd written for their new group.

"We've never sounded better," Sasha told her friends.

"That's what teamwork will do!" Jade agreed.

The evening rushed by in a blur of colors, lights, and music, and soon Mayor Davis was taking the stage one last time. The Super Starz climbed off the stage and stood with a big group of their friends in the audience. "Now for the moment you've all been waiting for," Mayor Davis began. "I am pleased to announce that the winners of this year's Best Costume awards are our very own Super Starz!"

The crowd cheered wildly as the band ran onstage once more. "Not only do they look like real pop stars, but they actually *became* stars on this stage here tonight," the mayor continued. "Now I'd say that's a successful costume!"

She presented each of the girls with a gold star on a pendant. "To remind you that you'll always be the stars of Stilesville," she explained. She even gave them an extra one to take back to Vinessa. "Now, would you girls like to say a few words?"

The six girls looked at each other, and then the friends all motioned Jade toward the microphone. "I just want to thank everyone for making this the best Halloween ever—until next year, anyway!"

The audience burst into cheers, and the Super Starz took their places to play one last song. The girls were happy to see the entire crowd on the dance floor, eager to enjoy every last moment of this fabulous Masquerade Ball.